Paradox

Stephen Evans

For the girls I knew in high school.

This is a work of fiction. The names, characters, places, and incidents are either the products of the author's imagination or are used fictitiously, and any resemblance to actual persons living or dead, business establishments, events, or locales is entirely coincidental.

Copyright © 2024 by Stephen Evans. All rights reserved.

Paradox/ Stephen Evans

ISBN: 978-1953725493

Contents

Red 1
White 3
Blue 41
Afterword 67
About the Author 69
Books by Stephen Evans 71

"He knew not what to do – something he felt, must be done – he rose, drew his writing-desk suddenly before him – sate down, took the pen – & found that he knew not what to do."

—Samuel Taylor Coleridge

Notebook, October 30, 1800

Red

In a moment.

He felt suspended. As if something was ready. So. Let it be.

The moment stretched.

He felt motion, but not focus. Nothing rose, took shape. This disturbed him.

Yet the moment did not dissipate. Instead the urge grew stronger.

He paced between piano and desk. He poured a drink, left it sitting. Again he moved, piano to desk to table to piano to desk.

He picked up a letter.

Love Always.

Baylor.

Stephen Evans

White

Baylor was not a fragile girl, though I could beat her two out of three in arm wrestling. So I was not completely surprised when she tackled me on the school lawn and sat looking down at me from a vantage point somewhere near my solar plexus.

Any normal person would have asked her why she had done it, but Baylor and I had passed that point long ago. I knew Baylor wasn't normal and I was beginning to have doubts about myself, a symptom of extreme Bayloritis due to overexposure.

Not that I minded. Sanity is a handicap in this world, ranking second only to intellect. Most of us have one or the other.

Baylor had the other.

There weren't many smarter than Baylor. There weren't many prettier either. She was without a doubt the single most extraordinary human in my graduating class.

The only mediocre thing about Baylor was me.

You see, I am not what you call your Class A type boyfriend. I'm not dumb and I'm not ugly, but compared to Baylor, well, there's no comparison. I am not in her galaxy. Suffice it to say that Baylor had her pick and she picked me and no one could figure out why, least of all me.

At first, I would ask her once a day, like vitamins. She would grow very quiet, move up close to me, look me in the eyes (she was exactly my height), put her arms around me—and then tickle me until I couldn't bear it.

This was about as responsive an answer as anyone ever managed to get out of Baylor. She suckered me every single time; she was a true hustler. In the artistic sense.

No wonder I loved her.

* * *

The first time we met was memorable, in that it was hardly the type of event you would expect to engender a loving relationship. She and I were on opposite sides of a debate in Mr. Butler's History class. The topic was capital punishment, I think. Anyway, I had prepared my case for weeks. I had a million quotes in evidence, and back copies of the Congressional Record covering the last thirty years.

I was ready.

I looked over at Baylor. She sat still and calm, seemingly unaware of her impending doom. I smiled in carnivore anticipation. When she looked back at me with those incredible eyes and a sweet smile spread slowly across her face, her tongue just barely visible between those equally incredible lips, I admit I began to feel remorseful. But, evidence was evidence. Logic was inescapable. Truth would out.

My throat felt strangely dry.

The bell rang, and Mr. Butler announced the topic. I stood at the podium and began to explain my case. My voice I admit was squeaky at first, though it grew stronger. I knew my stuff.

Ten minutes later, the class applauded as I returned to my seat. I had sweated through my jacket and was very glad to sit down.

Then Baylor got up.

The smile was gone from her face. There was a hint of effort in her chin. Her eyes. Her eyes. Sorry. Where was I? Oh yeah. Her eyes. They reminded me of a lamb. I saw one at a farm once when I was a kid. (Not that kind of kid.) As I looked into its eyes, it licked my nose. I consider this the central metaphor of my high school life.

Baylor walked gracefully to the podium without notes or evidence, but somehow I was not heartened. She surveyed her audience, smiled, and began.

There followed a thirty-minute extemporaneous annihilation of my case, complete with seven supreme court precedence citations for every one of mine. After two minutes, I acknowledged defeat. After five, I wished I could simply concede. After fifteen minutes, I began to envy the fates of Antony and Brutus. After twenty, I realized that even that would be anti-climactic. When she finished, I jumped to my feet with everyone else and joined the ovation in awe and admiration.

But not love.

Yet.

The class ended (KO in round one, the first of many) just as Mr. Butler was asking Baylor if her last name happened to be Cicero. I tried to sneak out without implying my existence but Baylor saw me and walked over, backing me into a corner (just as well, I needed the support).

"Sorry," she said, "I really liked your speech. I hope there are no hard feelings."

She seemed dismayed when I spent the next two minutes just staring at her. But I had never been this close to something so beautiful. Except that lamb. I wondered if she was going to lick my nose. This is how my mind was working.

As close as she was, her eyes and mouth seemed to cloud up the world. She pushed my glasses back on my nose, lifted my hand, and whispered in a voice so clear I knew everyone in school heard:

"I hope we can be friends."

I collected as much of myself as hadn't melted yet and stammered a y-y-yes. She squeezed my hand and turned to go and someone called out for her to wait and she turned around thinking it was me. (She told me this. I can't seem to remember it clearly.)

She stood there, waiting.

I tried to think of something to say.

I tried not to think of licking her nose.

"How did you memorize all those supreme court cases?" I asked finally.

"Oh those," she said, "I made them up."

Then.

Then it was love.

*   *   *

She grinned down at me from her clouds.

"I was just thinking about you."

"Have you noticed how often that involves physical violence?"

"Let's run off to Africa together."

"We can't. We have classes this afternoon."

"Not now, you idiot."

Baylor found communication with mere mortals frustrating. She sat back, relieving the pressure on my lungs, increasing it elsewhere.

When dealing with a Baylor sitting in a precarious position, I have found it best to play along, humor her wherever possible. A cowardly proposition, perhaps. Safer in the long run.

"Say when."

"Next week," she said.

She rolled off and lay next to me on the grass, our favorite juxtaposition. We often lay like this on hillsides in the country, watching the sky turn blue to pink to red to deeper blue. She would point out stars and constellations as if she knew them personally in all their quarks and idiosyncrasies.

"Well, if we can't go to Africa," she said, "let's at least take off tomorrow and go to Great Falls."

"Okay, I give up. Seduced to a life of crime. What will my mother say?"

"She'll say that if you and I are late for Physics one more time, we are going to get killed by Mr. Hinds."

* * *

"Evans, wake up. As for the rest of you clowns, I know you haven't read the chapter, so I'll just lecture for a while.

"Back in 1905, before some of you were born, an unknown patent examiner in Zurich was working almost completely alone on one of the most remarkable intellectual accomplishments in human history: The Theory of Relativity. I don't pretend to understand fully the entire theory, especially when the mathematics is very complex. The basic points, however, are relatively simple. Alright, quiet down, maybe you'll learn something.

"Imagine you are standing on a railway platform waiting to meet a friend. The train is struck by two bolts of lightning, one on the engine and one on the caboose. You see the lightning strikes simultaneously. But your friend on the train thinks the one that hit the engine is first. Who is right?"

I raised my hand.

Mr. Hinds looked skeptical but said "Yes?"

"If I am supposed to meet my friend, why is the train still moving."

He glared.

"This is Physics. You want backstory, wait for English class."

I shrugged.

"You have no idea."

"What?"

"I had no idea physics would be so interesting."

He almost smiled.

"Alright, use the rest of the period to finish up your lab reports, and try to get them in on time this time, okay?"

* * *

We started walking down the path to the falls. There was a large clearing at the end of the path, usually crowded even on Friday, with steel rails to keep the river from escaping, telescopes, and even a hot dog stand. All the comforts of the wilderness. Standing there you could see all the way upriver to the sunset. It looked just like a picture.

Baylor started pulling me along faster.

"Hey, come on, slow down, we're on a picnic, remember?"

She slowed a bit, her arm warm around my waist. Then suddenly, she turned and started off into the trees. By the time I caught up to her, she was standing with her back to a tree, watching me.

"Come on," she said, "I know a different way."

She took my hand. The undergrowth began to get dense, which was strange because the light through the trees was growing less and less bright, making diffused shadows on the rocks.

Clumps of dried debris clung to the trunks where years ago the river had flooded over. I tried to picture what it must have been like: no warning except a roar which by the time it was loud enough to warn would have been too near to escape. Animals standing: not running, afraid to move, fearing to release their place of momentary security; afraid not to move, fearing danger sensed but not known. Any human unlucky enough to see it was certainly long drowned.

Light broke, and almost blind we came on to the bank of a stream. It must have been a tributary of the river, though from where we stood we could see neither its beginning nor its end. It was not wide, but as swift and violent as the river was slow and tame farther downstream.

A bridge made of two ropes stretched over the stream: one for standing on, the other for clinging to for dear life. The ropes were connected on either side to two rotting oak trees and seemed to grow directly from the trees. The distance from water to bridge must have been at least thirty feet. The bridge led from nowhere to nowhere that I could see, but it was there and it was old.

Now I knew what Baylor was planning in her brilliant but demented little mind. But there was no way she was going to get me to cross that bridge. Absolutely no way. No way. So I said:

"Let me go across first. I swim better than you."

In spite of the fact that I was scared of heights, water, and drowning, I managed to edge my way across. Why the ropes held I do not know to this day. Rather proud of myself (I attribute my balance to the phenomenon of flat feet), I looked back at Baylor.

She wasn't smiling.

She wasn't even looking at me.

She was staring down into the surging foam.

Her eyes were unfocused, and the color of the water. The whole scene like watching an incomprehensible movie in an unknown language. I called to her, but softly, afraid of what would happen if I broke the spell. She looked up, surprised to see me there, unable to hear what I said.

She took one step onto the rope. All at once I was more afraid than I have ever been before or since, like walking into someone else's dream. I didn't know why, I didn't know how I knew, but I knew that Baylor was in danger from something I would never completely understand no matter how hard she would try to explain it to me, something I could see only through her.

"Baylor. Baylor, look at me. Don't look down. Just, look at me. Think about me. Alright. Slide your feet along slowly. Keep both hands on the rope. Easy. Good. Good."

As she stepped onto the bank, she collapsed, leaning her head on my shoulder. She was shaking. I put my jacket around her, which helped.

"I didn't know you were afraid of heights."

I didn't know she was afraid of anything.

"I'm not usually. I started listening to the water."

She shivered.

"Sometimes you just...need."

She lay back on the flat of the rock.

"I used to come here alone. Each time, I would get to a certain point, listen, and not be able to go on."

"What did you do?"

"I had to wait till it was almost dark. Then I could go back. Only back. It terrified me."

"Why did you keep coming back?"

Something flew once overhead, blocking out the sun.

* * *

"There was a young lady named Bright

"Whose speed was much faster than light.

"She set out one day

"In a relative way

"And returned on the previous night."

Mr. Hinds waited.

"Yes? No? Okay, turn to page 299,792."

* * *

I dribbled the ball down low, took the fifteen-foot jumper, then trotted back down the asphalt. She was laying in the sun, stretched out, a tawny cat. The halter top she was wearing almost made me forget the game. She never minded watching. I knew the other guys knew that she was there for me. It was a good feeling.

I grabbed the rebound, smiled at her as I ran down court. I took the ball, nodded left and spun to my right. Faked the pass, slipped under the basket and dunked the ball one-handed, behind my back.

In my mind.

* * *

The game had started late, so the cheerleaders were trying desperately to keep the crowd's spirits up. The crowd seemed to be enjoying himself, at least when he was awake. Normally I would have added to the cacophony of snores. However, at this particular game, I had found something to keep my interest.

She could jump nearly five feet off the ground, her legs split parallel, and all without effort, like a panther after prey. Her name was Baylor; she was in one of my classes. As I sat on the bench, I grew less and less interested in the game and more and more interested in her. Every time she looked over, I tried to appear an integral part of the action, hoping she would be impressed with my jock stature and school spirit. I think she found me out when I started cheering for both teams.

We were down by one point. They had the ball. I was sitting at the end of the bench, watching Baylor out of the corner of my eye. The coach, noticing my interest in the game, remembering my spectacular play in practice, walked down to me, tapped me on the shoulder.

"What's your name?"

"Jerry."

"You sure?"

"Yeah."

"You're in."

"Oh God."

I walked on to the court to the anthem of people rifling through their programs. 45? Who the hell is 45?

I asked the guy I replaced who he was guarding. He said he wasn't sure, that I should just lunge at who ever had the ball. This plan seemed incautious, so I decided to play my own little Zone defense, in which you stand in one place and yell Switch! whenever you can't find the man with the ball.

I was standing around minding my own business when this six-foot-twelve, three-hundred and ninety-pound monstrosity with a head like a basketball came charging up, and up, and up. I heard his wings flapping furiously.

A striped elf ran up, stood over my crushed and aching body, and pointed miraculously at the hulking brute burbling by the basket. I was helped off the court to the sound of thousands of cheering fans, was immediately signed to a pro contract of nine figures, and married the girl of my delusions.

Okay, we won by twelve and I never got in the game.

But I noticed her.

* * *

I came down off balance, twisted around, straining a million ligaments, pain screaming through my leg. As I was lying on the ground, my intense pain was superseded only by my excruciating humiliation.

Baylor ran over, very concerned, trying not to laugh.

"Does it hurt?"

"Ahhhhhhh."

"Guess it does."

I tried to get up, detected someone trying to reconnect my foot with a blowtorch, and immediately sat down, having deduced a causal connection.

Baylor was sitting as well by this time, doubled up in hysterics. There is something in people, the opposite of sadism, which makes them need to laugh at the strangest times. I don't know what it is or at least it's nothing I can say in words. Anyway, I was too busy laughing to think it through.

* * *

Warmth in darkness, closing round. The most relaxing experience ever devised by man. Alas for water bills. When I am President, I will order four showers per day for every man, woman, and child. Guaranteed to cut the crime rate fifty percent. Drownings up though. More work for the Coast Guard. Excuse me, Ma'am, didn't mean to barge in. Just making sure you weren't drowning. Yes, Ma'am, this is our official uniform. Let me help you into this life jacket.

Think I'll volunteer.

Dear Baylor,

Having a wonderful time.

Water is wonderful.

I am wonderful.

Everything is onederful.

Wish you were here.

Fish off a pier.

Gentlemen, place your bets.

Four point five four three billion to one that when I open my eyes the world will still be there.

All bets down?

Oh sorry, you lose.

Perhaps next time.

Tomorrow at sunrise.

Water looks at little rusty.

Must be picking up iron from the pipes.

Speak to Mother about that.

Shall I taste it?

The final draught before the final plunge.

It will make a new man out of you, Jekyll.

Shall I, Igor?

I must, or else I turn into Lon Chaney.

She always said she liked hairy chests.

Dear, before I marry you, there's something you should know.

Stand back. I, Snide Cartoon, will die in your place.

And now it is time to go; I to die and you to live.

All things which live must die.

All things to live must die.

Please pay at the rear.

Next please.

Ah, an excellent vintage.

Chateau Globulin, 1927.

Year of the Flood, according to Bishop Faulkner.

All you lymphocytes, step to the rear of the platelet.

I stepped out of the shower. The light was kind of funny; filtery and vague, like sunlight coming out of a cloud, I guess because of the steam in the room. Anyway, that's my excuse. I rammed my sprained foot, cast and all, into the toilet, exuding as I did so a long wailing cry to heaven (Goddamn stupid mother...) such as the prophets of old must have madeth in their scorn. Elijah and the children.

"Jerry?"

My father has arisen. Speaking of bears.

"I'm alright, Dad. I hurt my foot."

"Your mother told me about that. Pretty stupid, don't you think, Jer?"

"Thanks, Dad."

"That's okay, son, your mother and I, we accept you as you are."

"Swell, Dad."

"Try not to make so much noise, Son."

"I'll try, Dad."

"Your mother tells me that you are going out with this Baylor girl again. Are you seeing her?"

"Yes, Dad."

"Oh. Well, that's fine, Son. You have a nice time."

So much for childhood.

* * *

"I'll drive," she said.

Immediately I started to argue but stopped when I saw the look on her face. Anyway she was right.

That is a maddening habit she has sometimes. There are times in a person's life when she should be scrupulously wrong. Baylor never was. It wasn't her fault, I guess, though sometimes I neglected to acknowledge that fact, mostly because when she was right she inevitably became stubborn, the case of an all-too-stoppable force against an object not immovable yet so convinced of its immobility that even when you moved it you could never force it to recognize that fact, which in the end made the entire effort not worthwhile.

But I couldn't drive safely with this cast on my leg. And once in a while Baylor drove sanely. So I let it go.

I got in the car, buckled my seat belt, mumbled a silent prayer, and sulked while Baylor got in.

"Hey Jerry."

I looked up just in time to keep from being inundated by 120 pounds of pouncing girl. Some minutes later (I wasn't counting), I managed to fill my lungs. The problem with Baylor is not getting a word in, it's getting a word out.

"You crushed your corsage."

"It's fine. You have terrible taste anyway."

"Drive the car."

"By the way, I love your boot."

"Just drive the car."

"I'm driving."

To my intense satisfaction and no little amazement, Baylor became very quiet, as if she sensed that she had gone too far, or maybe she was just acting the role, or maybe... her craziness will drive me crazy.

"Do you have the tickets?"

"Yes."

"Don't lose them."

"Baylor."

It's amazing the way her retreats end in total victory.

* * *

I picked her up at seven-thirty. Well, almost seven-thirty. I was late. To tell the truth I wasn't all that sure that I wanted to go. At least, I knew I didn't want to arrive on time.

Any time you arrive on time to a party, you are early. Don't ask me why, I don't understand it either; it's the archetypal social mythos of western civilization. If you arrive on time, you are invariably the first, which is not only embarrassing, since the host is never expecting you that early, but it also places an inordinate social responsibility on the guest, who becomes charged with getting the party started right. Many times, Baylor has rescued me from that cruel task. She has a flair for sociology.

"I told you that you didn't have to come if you didn't want to."

"Does that mean I can turn around?"

It's amazing how imperious a simple raised eyebrow can be.

"I wouldn't let you go by yourself anyway."

She glanced at me, her lips edging into a curious smile.

"I didn't think you had it in you."

"What?"

"Jealousy."

"I just like to be cautious. Baylor, I can't concentrate when you do that."

"Chicken."

"Exactly. Why don't we go someplace private and discuss it?"

"Because we were invited to a party."

"I could be sick. You could tell him you were nursing me back to health. I know the perfect therapy."

"No."

"If we don't have to go, I promise I'll take you to Africa? Asia? Mars? My place?"

"I can't understand why you don't like parties."

"I like parties—it's people I can't stand."

"I'm serious."

I sighed.

"Baylor, you know exactly what happens when I go to a party with you. I end up tagging along while you discuss Nietzschean pyrotechnics. Not that I'm not fascinated by pyrotechnics, it's just that I'd rather practice than preach."

"Jerry, my driving instructor always recommended watching while you drive."

"I'll bet I know what he was watching, too. If we can turn around, I'll marry you. That's my final offer."

"You really don't want to go, do you? Too late, we're here."

"Lishen, Schweetheart, I can ditch de car. We'll be in Canada by morning. They'll never take us alive."

"Cary Grant, right? Come on."

I was trapped.

We walked up to the door.

Last chance.

She rang the bell.

Damn.

Oh well.

The door opened.

I consider myself a rather laconic person, not given to over-emotionalism. But when some guy picks up the girl who you are pretty sure is your girl, kisses her in a distinctly unplatonic, faintly European way, and starts to carry her off, something has to be done. I accept a certain amount of absurdity in my life as inherent to Baylor's nature, but you have to draw the line somewhere or things get out of hand. Or in hand, as the case may be. So I said casually:

"Excuse me, I believe you picked up my girl by mistake."

It was either that or a karate chop to the base of the spine. As soon as I said it, I knew I had chosen wrong.

"Oh, hi, Jerry, when did you get here? No, it was no mistake, I assure you."

He was about six foot two.

Blue eyes.

Had to turn sideways to fit his shoulders through the door.

Hell of a nice guy.

I hated him.

I had read somewhere that mustaches like that were indicative of sexual impotence.

And Baylor.

She lay there just as if she enjoyed it.

As if.

"Oh, don't worry about it, John. Just put her back in my car when you finish with her. Oh hi, Suzanne."

After about half an hour of mingling, I took my accustomed place in the corner by the stereo. Actually, standing in a corner is one of the most intriguing things you can do at a party. You have an excellent vantage from which to view the goings-on. You can watch the people laugh, talk, smile, stare. The music is close. A bowl of peanuts is invariably within reach. The advantages are numerous.

Also, your flank is protected, an important tactical advantage.

When you stand in the corner for some time, you achieve a semi-institutional status. People come and ask you all sorts of questions like "why are you standing in a corner?" They never believe you are having fun. I have two stock answers for that question, depending on the sex of the enquirer and the extent of my alcoholic intake:

1) I've been waiting for you to come over and talk to me.

2) I can't stand up anywhere else.

Baylor, of course, was her usual sensational self. I never really got around to watching anyone but her. I guess you never realize how much you wish you could fly until you're falling off a cliff.

I ate too many peanuts.

I hate parties.

I hate people who hate parties.

Why am I so stupid?

Why can't I just walk up to her and say I'm sorry?

She'd probably laugh at me.

She's having a great time.

I bet she doesn't even remember me.

I looked up.

She was there.

"Hi, my name's Baylor. I was lonely and you looked lonely too so I thought I'd come and talk to you. You remind me of this guy I'm in love with. I'd go talk to him, but I think he's mad at me, so..."

Kissing someone at a party always draws attention. Sometimes I love an audience.

* * *

"All right, everybody, listen. We're going to play a little game."

Massive inward groans. Suzie's games are invariably dumb or disastrous.

"Experiment in extra-sensory perception. Everyone come over here. Sit in a circle around the candle."

Light's out.

"Everyone join hands. Okay, watch the candle. Clear your mind and try to reach out to the other people in the circle. Pick up their thoughts, feelings, whatever."

So I'm a human radio. Hello. Hello. Are you out there?

hellothisisalitlegreenman

Baylor's, warm in left.

Suzie right, pressing on my thigh.

Should say something.

Wax streaks down the candle.

Completely arbitrary.

Beauty simply... chance?

No.

Only seems.

I know.

Focus on the point.

Flame.

Flicker.

Warmth.

Leaking down.

Into.

Around.

My kingdom for a cause.

Settle into Baylor's hand.

Cold now.

Look over.

Baylor.

Eyes glinting.

Candle shadow swallowed by the darkness in the room.

Vampiress?

Squeeze her hand.

Staring.

Baylor?

Baylor?

Connect.

She straightens up.

Eyes now wide.

Circle broken.

Silent staring back.

Her other hand moved slowly down toward mine.

Jerry?

Baylor.

Touch.

Blackness endless falling surrounding lost sinking into sucking down a vacuum void unending life lost Baylor no.

No.

Won't.

Let.

Flicker.

Light.

"Light. Turn on the lights."

Brightness surged into the room. Baylor, tears streaking, looked at me.

"Take me home."

*   *   *

I opened the door, stared out on the rain grey streets. To home or where. Home is where...you hang your heart. Profound.

We walked out, as I tried to hold my jacket over her head, my arm around her shoulder. Protectionist contortions. Baylor turned and grinned at me. Off she spun and ran into the rain. Salt rain safer there:

"No way, Rene. No way, Rene."

But I don't think she believed it.

The moment of intensest life is the taste of a rain wet girl.

* * *

I didn't really know what was wrong at first. I looked over through the candle, superficially trying to think of words but really trying to think, to find, to uncover something much more astounding, more insidious than mere words. Her face, her voice, her gestures were all blank; here was a girl I thought I knew well enough to love, loved well enough to... what? I didn't know. I felt the box in my pocket, the ribbon probably crushed, if not by Baylor's escapade in the car then at least by my constantly checking to see if it was there, all in place and ready. The candle flickered, her face in shadow, disguising what was not even there.

I felt like Pygmalion in reverse, suddenly seeing the living breathing loving girl whom I loved turn into an artifact without design or meaning. Never before had I been unable to read at least a little of Baylor's thought: in her body, the way she sat, or walked, even if it was only what she wanted me to read and even if only through her eyes which had no glitter now not even a candle's reflection.

Any action I made now would be wrong, possibly disastrous, yet not to act, to relinquish the will, ability, desire to act would be to abandon whatever hold we have on life through each other I think or something and I really should think these things out ahead of time since I am no good in the moment we know that about me but whether or not through some unforeseen event wherein we might possibly manage to scrape through this time it is certain or nearly certain that there would come a time when action would be both necessary and if I failed now impossible so no choice would be the worst I think choice of all I hope or something like that.

"Baylor?"

"Yes."

As if she made no sound at all.

"I have something for you."

"Please don't."

"I have to."

I took the box out of my pocket, handed it to her. It was small, wrapped in silver paper (by the lady in the jewelry shop—I never could wrap presents), with the silver ribbon slightly crushed. I didn't realize till then that she must have noticed it in the car, must have felt its size, must have been wondering furiously, fearfully, what it was. Perhaps she even slid her hand inside my pocket and felt the ribbon, the size of the box.

Suddenly, I knew.

I laughed.

"Open it."

"Will you tell me what it is first?"

"It's a present. By the way, what's your ring size?"

"Oh God, Jerry. Jerry, I love you, I really do, more than I could ever...but I couldn't possibly... I... it ...please take it back? Please?"

"I want you to open it."

Seeing Baylor at that moment, I can imagine Odysseus, trapped at last, leaving home and family for a war which he doesn't want to fight in a place from which he may never return and certainly will never return unchanged. Slowly she took the package and slowly opened it, watching my eyes for a phone call from the Governor. It never came.

She lifted the lid, looked quickly at me, then down. She pulled away the cotton. I think the room began to glow, a slow milky white. Her face screwed up. Her eyes went nova: an astral vision.

She threw back her chair, almost tripping on the carpet, and leaped into my lap, spilling the few remaining drops of wine in my glass.

"Help me with it."

I reached for it, drew the silver chain around her neck, kissed the oval lanced with a silver cross made especially for her it, where it hung between her breasts.

*   *   *

On the roof.

"So?" I asked.

"In time."

"And?"

"Yes."

"Then?"

"Of course."

I paused, then nodded.

"Well okay then."

We lay back together.

"Are the stars coming towards us or away?"

She smiled.

"Always."

Blue

To kingdom comes the woman, rapt in mist,
dawning graceful on the festive stage,
attentive, as she makes her way
(glissando) to the legendary King.
Reflecting future passed within her glance –
triadic radiation of her soul,
a furnace of infernal paradise,
transmutation's cold transcendency,
sacred stairs between the stars
– she stares transfixed.

Her open mouth can echo but the peal,
celestial chimes, in magic climbing thirds.
The Ten spoke from her pyramid.
Frozen, sweeping through the darkened hall,
here, no words.

Fire leapt up to meet the impassive challenge,
blind ascendancy of mindless calm,

*and yet still frozen eyelids of the Knights
twitched in fear of timeless loss of fear,
unable yet to glance each other's way.
Even Arthur, stricken on his throne,
awe over-riding all his childlike frame,
huge, graven image of nobility
such as ancient pharaohs loved to bear
in death, he seemed; and yet he strove
unlike his Knights, with tempered might,
to break the spell she cast upon the whole.*

*It was only then that brave Sir Lancelot,
miraculous, true hearted, famous night,
stumbled in his grace upon the hall
bewitched by her bewitched.
"Your Majesty," said he, "your pardon
for my entering so late.
An errand for which my honor bore no wait
had drawn me thence."*

He paused before his silent friend.
"I beg you, sire, speak some word to me.

Condemn me with your welcome Majesty,
but be not mute."

Only then did Lancelot perceive
the silence spread throughout the darkened Hall.
His eye fell on the woman still,
priestess captive of the song,
unwilling siren, bound as those she bound.
Straight he strode unto the woman,
Threw back her hood and looked upon her face.
He gazed into the nothing of her mind,
Saw the lineless beauty of her youth,
Gray-eyed maiden carven to a masque.
He placed his hand upon her throat
white it was as her white gown,
he felt the lifeless pulse beneath her flesh,
and sighed that beauty should so cruelly die.

Then then fell he back, pierced by sudden light;
brightness blazing from the lady's eyes,
an eerie glimmer growing to great size
and taking shape as though it were alive.

Huge it grew, filling all the Hall,
rafters cracking from its outstretched wings,
a single soulful call was heard,
shrill trumpet of the passing life beyond.
Incarnate lightning took it for its form,
and all save Lancelot cowered in its glance.
Two shapeless hands it lifted as in prayer,
then parted, blue electric singing force,
creating there a vision far away.
Through time and space the creature's vision passed,
unmindful of the universal law,
until it came to rest upon the Grail.

Chaos filled the faces of the Knights,
forced to rise were mind can never dwell.
A blinding madness seized some frozen few,
and ne'er they looked again save in great fear.

A mighty man of miracles,
brave Sir Lancelot once more strode,
not towards the raging cold colossal thing,

but towards the woman, thrall source of its power.
His feet grew heavy and he knew great fear,
but to his fear Du Lac could never yield.
He reached the trembling, shattered, standing form,
and with his two great hands he shut her eyes.
The creature fell and vanished in a fog
whichever more lay shimmering on the heath
surrounding Caerleon, castle of the King.
The woman swooned and met her proper death,
and Lancelot was driven to his knees

Soon the terror of the vision passed
and all the Hall was filled with wondrous clamber.
Arthur bore Sir Lancelot to his bed
and tended him till the coming of the Queen

"Well," said Sir Kay, Arthur's Seneschal,
"I wot well that we finally may eat!"

Long Sir Lancelot lay upon his bed.
Sore his heart was pressed by forms unseen
and poured he forth strange solemn muttering.

Often cried he out into the night,
Mortal shrieks that pierced the very walls
into the chambers of the king and queen.
Surgeons found they none could aid him
nor holy men relieve his suffering.
Therefore said the King unto the Queen,
"I fear our faithful friend is lost.
No medicine can be found to save him.
O where is Merlyn when we need him most."

A silent rush of air surrounded them,
as if a door had opened into Night.
"Here as always in your time of need."
So said the voice which circled the dark.
"Merlyn!" said Arthur, very much surprised,

"Now, now, Arthur, don't upset yourself.
It happens that I'm very much asleep.
It's simply that I placed you in my dream.
So tell me, Arthur Lad, what's happening?
Sorry, that's a youthful idiom."

And so related Arthur all that tale
of the miraculous Pentecostal feast
and the valor of Sir Lancelot,
and the sorry plight of that good knight.
Silence rose about the room
and whistled to itself. While Merlyn thought,
the king looked at his much-loved queen with hope.

"I cannot help you, Arthur," said the Voice,
"but do not fear, because you need no help.
Thirty days and seven and yet two,
Lancelot will lie upon his bed.
On the final day he will arise
and you will see the light within his eyes.

At that time he will undertake a quest.
He will conceive the strangest project
ever imagined...to become a knight errant
and sally forth into the world
to right all wrongs, to find the Sangreal.
I'm very sleepy, Arthur, there's no more
I can tell you anyway. Good night."

"Wait! Merlyn! Will he succeed or not?
May we yet lose the brave Sir Lancelot?"
Answer came there none.
So instead, the King and Guinevere returned to bed.

The Day foretold, Sir Lancelot appeared
and knelt before the King and Queen.
He begged his leave with calming words
knowing well their fears for him.

"By what is right I am compelled
to venture forth in search of beauty's flame
and wisdom's fire and truth's enduring light.
I cannot now forsake this quest,
creation, which has burned into my mind,
flashing visions of my life
alone amidst the cold eternal stars.
The silent music of the universe
calls to me, and I shall never rest
until I finally embrace the source.
And so I ask your leave, my dearest friends.

Thoughts of you I'll carry on my way
and hope it last to see you once again.
But whether hope shall pass no man can say,
or, if it stay, no man can reckon when."

Saying thus, he bowed before the King,
who wondered at his gladness for his friend.
(What man can know he wants his friend to
cherished be in memory?)
Then he knelt before the Queen, his love.
"Go," she said and held him with her eyes,
and feared she not to cry to keep him there.
No words, he said unto her heart,
"I leave you, maybe not to come again."

She sighed, her strength enfolding her heart,
and carefully swept the shards of love away
into some sheltered corner till he returned.

Star wandered far Sir Lancelot through time
undifferentiated by light or night.
He lost his sense of East or West.

The unending dawn could have been dusk,
For often the eye tricks in uncertain light.
Life for Lancelot grew burdensome,
carrying ever the weight of hope.
The vision took possession of his mind;
where e'er he looked he caught a fleeting glimpse
of that eternal founding font of light.

He passed into a country like his home.
Weary and sore both in mind and heart,
he paced beside his great, white steed
high into the mountains like his own.

To rest his horse, he stopped beside a pool
beside a rock wind carven skull-like stone.
Two web-footed, flat-billed birds walked calmly by,
seeming to disappear between the rocks.
Intrigued, Lancelot followed in their path,
and came upon the entrance to a cave.

Dark into the mountain ran the stone,
strangely smooth yet emanating steam
A man who wanders far has less to lose,
yet even Lancelot, valiant knight,
felt fear within the queer, trembling draft
issuing from the hidden opening.
Yet an underlying sense of joy,
of quest fulfilled, conquered Lancelot.
Down he sprang, swallowed by the dark,
chill upon his entering, the wind.

Time lost dwelt in the murky lair.
Hours, maybe, Lancelot, spiraling
round the cavern ways, walked blind,
keeping ever the wind upon his face.

Light like a physical force upon his eyes
leapt suddenly, striking him blinder than before.
He stopped, adjusting his mind to the atmosphere.
When finally his vision cleared,
he saw it standing, golden, far away.
Not that vision which his heart most sought,

but another nearly as wondrous in its way.

*Rising far above an arid plane,
a tower rose leagues into the air.
The massive edifice of ancient splendor
glowed with a magnificent radiance.
So brilliant was the light which shone,
so powerful the heat of that great work,
the Valley had become a desert furnace,
deadly to any who dared pass its gates.*

*Upon the tower four great golden wings
slowly revolved, powered not by wind.
The sun itself poured waves of energy
over that vast and whirling hand,
turning in silence, inexorably,
inscribing infinite patterns in the air,
up and down and slowly out and in,
in endless revolution.*

*"A Sunmill!" Lancelot cried in awe and joy.
Yet, as the light reflected everywhere,*

bouncing off hill and mountain, rock and plain,
Lancelot imagined that he saw the light
not entering in but surging from the tower,
igniting with its blaze even the Sun.

No more could Lancelot restrain his heart,
bursting in gladness, madness darting in,
he stumbled down the mountain in his haste.
Stepping on the plain, the bitter heat
drenched him with fatal, life-sapping caress.
And yet, a man who glories in his soul
over some sudden, all-enchanting find
cares little for his body's suffering
while he pursues the image in his mind.
And so it was for lofty Lancelot
drawing all the terrors of his quest,
and now, his mind full filled by his dream's rest,
he hardly knew his body held his joy.

No other man, perhaps, could have endured
the pounding pressure of relentless light,
and still retained his motion, life, and sight.

Lancelot never faltered once in step,
never doubted once in mind or heart,
already seemed inhuman in his might.

Enthralled, he then drew near the monolith,
and stood abashed. No shadow did it cast,
no shade of normal substance entered
that vast and empty sea of ash,
not even that of Lancelot Du Lac.

Lancelot closed his eyes before the sight
And still the image stood before his mind,
as though the light could pierce all mortal veils.
Suddenly, his mind was lifted up,
soaring high, far above the plane.
Looking down from that immortal height,
the monolith appeared a bloody eye,
vast in shimmering red as setting sons.

And yet amid that strange and wondrous space,
the strangest sight of all soon met his eyes.
A cackling noise rose in that silent place,

startling him and drawing back his mind.
He opened his eyes and saw three aged men,
elders of the human race, dancing about,
jumping up and down, screaming and roaring,
waving their arms around, whirling about,
circling over the sand,
the three old men made their way towards him.

"Halt, old men. Explain your silly game."
The three men gasped and fell down in surprise.
Two whispered to one another amid curious sighs.
The eldest simply looked at Lancelot.

"Do you not tremble at our ferocious smile?"
called the white-haired lonely one.

"We shall devour you, stranger. You must run."
So said the dark and thin, bespeckled one.
The eldest of them never said a word,
but turned and walked towards the tower.

The two old men, grimacing in the sand,

shook their heads and followed in this trail.
Lancelot, wondering if his mind was parched,
loosened his sword and trudged on after them.
So he came under the magic door,
which else he never would have found,
being but a simple man of truth.

Passing through the door he found the Hall,
larger than Arthur's Hall at Caerleon.
The room was shaded and was very cool
after the Inferno roundabout.
They sat around the table, long and square,
and made of purest marble, and they stared,
until the eldest rang a bell.

The bell rang hollow in the empty hall.
At the further end, another rang,
a tiny silver bell, or so he thought,
and yet it seemed a figure rose from there,
ghostly white, gliding over the floor.
At once Sir Lancelot sprang upon his feet.
He drew his sword and backed against the wall,

fearing another onslaught from the thrall,
the nightmare creature which
had spawned his dream.

The white-haired old one stood and laughed,
"what sort of knight is this who fears a maid,
a tender maid of meek, uncertain air?"
Again he laughed, and both the others too,
but wise Sir Lancelot did not look or move,
but kept his gaze upon the shining girl.

"Such a maiden have I seen before.
I sought to save her then, but still she died.
Is this not then some phantom of the mind,
a vengeful spirit who will take all our lives?"

The three old men took counsel once again.
The dark one lowered his spectacles and said,
"the girl you see before you now is real,
the other must have been the counterfeit.
Elaine is daughter to our age.

Yet all this I think you will know well.
But tell us of yourself, what travels passed,
mysterious wanderer from beyond this realm?"

"Tell us how you saw through our disguise.
We are the guardians of the monolith,
and many have we frightened from its doors.
Our best illusion is of Kerberus,
and yet you knew us, three old foolish men."

"Foolish you are, but I love you still."
The silver voice flowed pure into his heart,
and Lancelot now perceived a different joy.

Much passed between the lovers for a time.
It is not strange that they fell in love,
being alone and fair and true and young.
Not uncommon was their love,
for all their strange and wondrous dwelling place.
Yet Lancelot felt he had forgotten
something his heart could never rest without.
Lancelot never was too bright,

and love had now submerged his other dream.
The idyll lasted for another month,
and Lancelot grew in strength and health and love.

Happiness would not come to Lancelot.
Elaine and he were puzzled by his gloom.
He had all things that other men desire,
or so it seemed, in their first innocence.

He spoke to the old men about his thoughts.
"Why am I not happy in this place?
I feel desires tugging at my heart,
luring me, singing me in some wild tongue.
What must I do to be as other men?"

All of them were sad. The time had come.
So spake the silent one to Lancelot.
"Seldom do I deign to speak to men.
What I had to say has long been said
on earth, and none can tell it better even now.
But this I will say, Lancelot, son of Ban,
Knight of Arthur's table at Caerleon.

Beyond those golden doors there is a stair.
Leagues uncounted winds it up the tower.
Terrors guard the way, such as you
have never faced. But fear them not.
They were meant for lesser men than you.
At the very top of this great stair,
another room exists. It has one light,
lit in the depths of time.
In this room I know that you shall find
the true desire of your heart and mind."

"Will you not try to stop me if I go?"

But the eldest would not speak again.
So, the frosty had one answered next.
"We are old men. What power have we
to guard against a mighty knight like you?
We do not guard this fortress, anyway.
We only seek to keep unwary souls
from facing the terrors of the tower
unaware and unprepared.
Few who see that sight will e'er return."

Then spoke the girl, in sorrow, beautiful.
"Lancelot, I beg you, stay with me.
We shall find our dual destiny."

Lancelot smiled absently, and turned,
"I shall see and then I shall return."

Lancelot walked out upon the stair.
Climbing, passed he all the feeble ghosts
And other traps to catch unworthy men.
Behind him follow sounds of sage advice.
First, the dark one's sharp voice echoes up:
"No gods are heroes. Only men are heroes."
Then, the grumbly voice of the frosty one:
"Earth's the right place for love.
I don't know where it's likely to go better."
Silence closed behind him as he walked.

Even to such as Lancelot,
great hearted, bold, and passionate knight
such as he had even been in youth,

there comes at times a fit of mastery.
Then, earthly barriers had best give way,
for nothing on earth can hold them from their goal.
In Lancelot, such mastery had grown
so far the sun itself was not his match.
The dormant power of his naïve mind
asserted itself within his genius ways.
His vision grew then powerful and clear,
so even matchless light would fear his sway.

Once at the top, he strode into the room,
brushing aside the ghosts that barred his path
by the human fire in his mind.
On a throne of mist there stood the Grail,
at once the source of all the world's light.
Form of cup, yet formless, full
and empty all at once it seemed.
"I see but with my eyes!" cried Lancelot.
Longing tore like vultures at his soul.
"I see, I see, that I shall never see.
Who could endure to be a man
if that which is most precious is denied.

Man I'll be no more."

Blankly moved his body towards the Grail,
if now it could be said to have a place.
Fire leapt up around it, lacking heat.
Unconsumed, the burnished metal blazed
higher and higher with Lancelot's every step,
as if it hungered fiercely to devour.

At the door, stricken, stood the girl,
armored in the whiteness of her shift,
now red as flame, and silver pendant
hanging close between her breasts.
Even amid all that tumultuous rage,
a miracle occurred midst miracles.
Simple it was, of human scope,
yet miracle even so. Lancelot turned.

He saw the awesome beauty of her fear,
and knew the fear was for himself not her,
and something in his heart began to crack,
crumble under passion's strain

whose fury matched that in his sight.
A man can stand so much for love,
but once he loves two opposites too much,
his heart will break e're he could ever choose;
thus are great men made and thus destroyed.
Remembering the fire in her eyes
as she stood in the ruin of the door,
he chooses her and still he moves away,
unsure if he is drawing or is drawn.

Once more he looks at her, once more the flame,
sees once more the fire in her eyes,
he looks on her live beauty challenging him
to dare to be himself and still he looks,
until the fibers of his heart snap,
his eyes caught by silver flashing red.
As her breasts pulse up and down,
he sees the Grail reflected in her chain
and pendant, shining forth in crimson waves,
and once the spell redoubled captures him
but now both vision and reality
draw him to the woman he must love.

Taking her hand, his back still to the blaze,
he leaves the room and sits upon the stair,
kissing pendant and woman still and fair,
he sets the door ajar,
and carries his love far from the shining glare.

"Won't Arthur be surprised!" he said to her.
I went to find a Grail and found a girl."

STEPHEN EVANS

Afterword

I'm pretty sure I wrote the first complete version of this story in college. The middle part, *White*, might have been written in high school.

I submitted *White* to *Mademoiselle* magazine, back then a well-known venue for stories, and received an encouraging note from the editor asking for more stories, which I didn't have. If I had known then how significant that invitation was, I might have paid more attention and my writing career could have been very different. But I didn't, so it wasn't.

High school was a good time in my life. I made friends that I have kept for fifty-some years. Some part of my enjoyment of this story surely comes from the high school memories incorporated into the middle section *White*. Jerry isn't me—I was the brilliant one in high school. But he has better luck with girlfriends than I did. Possibly those two are connected.

Whatever faults you (or I) may find with it now, this story has elements (style, humor, philosophy) consistent with nearly everything I have written since. So, either I have learned nothing over the years, or I have been writing from my true self. I prefer the later explanation (though not discounting the former), and take some comfort in that continuity. I hope you enjoyed those elements at least, as I continue to do.

About the Author

Stephen Evans is a playwright and the author of *The Island of Always, Whose Beauty is Not Changed*, and *Funny Thing Is: A Guide to understanding Comedy*.

Find him online at:

https://www.istephenevans.com/

https://www.facebook.com/iStephenEvans

https://twitter.com/iStephenEvans

STEPHEN EVANS

Books by Stephen Evans

Fiction:

The Island of Always:
   The Marriage of True Minds
   Let Me Count the Ways
   My Winter World
The Marriage Gift
Paradox
Whose Beauty is Past Change
The Mind of a Writer and other Fables
Some Version of This is Funny: Assorted Epigrammaticon
The Next Joy and the Next

Non-Fiction:

Funny Thing Is: A Guide to Understanding Comedy
Prolegomena to Any Future Vacation
Layers of Life
Liebestraum
The Laughing String: Thoughts on Writing

Stephen Evans

Plays:

The Visitation Quartet:
  The Ghost Writer
  Monuments
  Tourists
  Spooky Action at a Distance
At the Still Point

Experience	*Three plays about Ralph Waldo Emerson*
Generations	*(with Morey Norkin and Michael Gilles)*
As You Like It	*(by William Shakespeare, adapted by Stephen Evans)*
The Glass Door	*(An adaptation of Hedda Gabler by Henrik Ibsen)*

Verse:

Limerosity
Limerositus
Sonets from the Chesapeke
The Crooked Mirror

PARADOX 73

STEPHEN EVANS

Paradox 75

STEPHEN EVANS